ANIMAL POEMS

Chosen by Brian Moses

Illustrated by Natalia Moore

WINDMILL
BOOKS

Published in 2018 by **Windmill Books**, an Imprint of Rosen Publishing
29 East 21st Street, New York, NY 10010

Editor: Victoria Brooker
Designer: Lisa Peacock

Acknowledgments: The Compiler and Publisher would like to thank the authors for allowing their poems to appear
in this anthology. Poems © the authors. While every attempt has been made to gain permissions and provide an
up-to-date biography, in some cases this has not been possible and we apologise for any omissions. Should there be
any inadvertent omission, please apply to the Publisher for rectification.

"The Terrible Ten!" by James Carter taken from "I'm A Little Alien!" by James Carter (Janetta Barry Books/
Frances Lincoln) copyright @ 2014;"Komodo Dragon" first appeared in Wild! Rhymes That Roar, chosen by James
Carter and Graham Denton, Macmillan Children's Books, 2009; "A Bear in his Underwear" by Brian Moses, taken
from "The Monster Sale" (Frances Lincoln) 2013; "How to Spot a Kangaroo" from "Snail Stampede and Other
Poems" by Robert Scotellaro (Hands Up Books, 2004).

Cataloging-in-Publication Data
Names: Moses, Brian.
Title: Animal poems / compiled by Brian Moses.
Description: New York : Windmill Books, 2018. | Series: Poems just for me | Includes index.
Identifiers: ISBN 9781499483895 (pbk.) | ISBN 9781508193203 (library bound) | ISBN 9781508193128 (6 pack)
Subjects: LCSH: Animals--Juvenile poetry. | Children's poetry, American. | Children's poetry, English.
Classification: LCC PS595.A5 A52 2018 | DDC 811.6--dc23

Manufactured in China
CPSIA Compliance Information: Batch #BS17WM: For Further Information contact Rosen Publishing, New York, New York at 1-800-237-9932

Contents

The Terrible Ten!

One!
Do a *stroll* like a tiger

Two!
Do a *grrr* like a bear

Three!
Do a *scuttle* like a spider

Four!
Do a *leap* like a hare

Five!
Do a *stretch* like a lion

Six!

Do a *flap* like a bat

Seven!

Do a *swoop* like a barn owl

Eight!

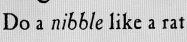

Do a *nibble* like a rat

Nine!

Do a *sway* like an eagle

Ten!

Do a *waddle* like a hen

Then it might be nice
just once or twice
to do the ten again!

James Carter

On My Way from School

On my way from school I saw a cat
It was a fat cat
It was a black, fat cat
It was a big, black, fat cat
It was a hairy, big, black, fat cat
It was a scary, hairy, big, black, fat cat
It was a mean, scary, hairy, big, black, fat cat
It was *my* mean, scary, hairy, big, black, fat cat
   called Cuddles
And she followed me home.

Roger Stevens

Animal Riddles

It has four hooves, a tail of course.
Who wants to ride this lovely ...

It's dressed in feathers, rhymes with carrot
sharp curved beak, must be a ...

It's long, and skinny as a rake.
Don't let it bite, must be a ...

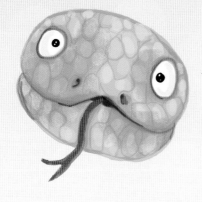

It's small and scuttles round the house.
A long, thin tail, must be a...

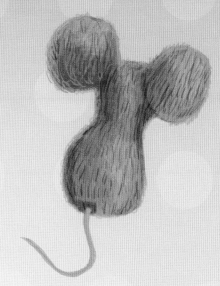

Long ears, bright eyes, a hopping habit,
round white tail, must be a...

You count them when you're trying to sleep.
Those woolly jumpers, must be...

Marian Swinger

9

My Dog

My dog is cuter
than a baby snuggling with a teddy bear.

My dog is naughtier
than a boy putting a rat in his teacher's handbag.

My dog is fluffier
than a bed made out of cotton wool.

My dog is braver
than a medieval knight riding into battle.

My dog is sillier
than a clown doing a backflip with his pants down.

My dog eats more
than a Tyrannosaurus at a buffet.

My dog barks louder
than the eruption of twenty volcanoes.

But enough about that —
you should see my cat!

Joshua Seigal

Sad Rabbit

How they fussed over me
When I was new:
Filled up my bowl —
Played with me too.
Fed me green leaves,
Dandelions and such,
Stroked my long ears,
Cleaned out my hutch.
Life was great then
But gradually
They found other things
And lost interest in me.
They had new bikes, a football,
A computer to use —
A sad, lonely rabbit
Was yesterday's news.
Now they don't even
Bother to come.

Who brings my food?
Not them, but their Mum.
She says, "It's your rabbit,
It's really not fair.
It needs a new home
And someone to care."
So perhaps I'll be moving
To someone quite new
Who'll care for a rabbit —
What about you?

Eric Finney

A Bear in His Underwear

You shouldn't point and you mustn't stare
if you see a bear in his underwear.

It's really rude to take a peep
at a bear just woken from winter sleep.

A bear who's out to test the air
while wondering what clothes to wear.

For him it will be a big surprise,
he'll be trying to rub the sleep from his eyes.

He'll be thinking of honey and hoping to find
something sweet that the bees left behind.

So don't be surprised if when you wave
he disappears into his cave.

He'll really be in no mood to talk
till he's properly dressed and off for a walk.

So if you see a bear with holes in his vest
and pants a long way past their best,

Pass him by — just leave him there,
if you see a bear who's almost bare!

Brian Moses

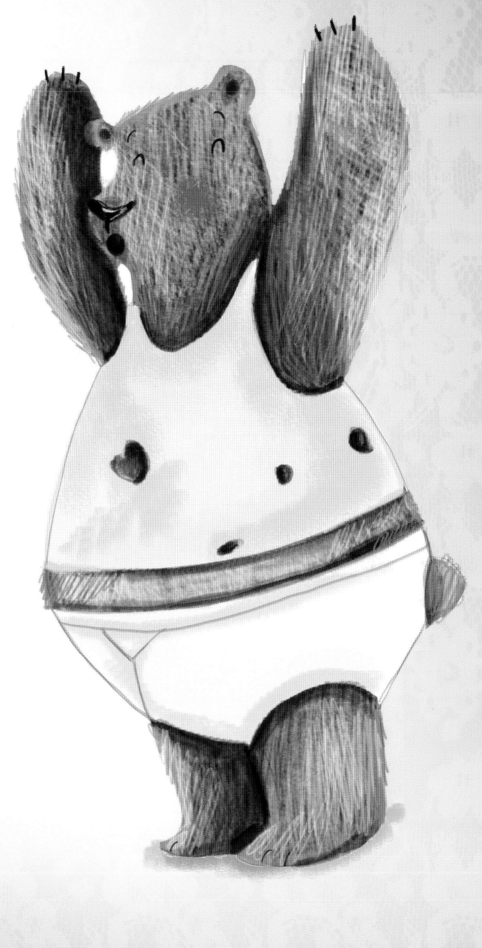

Komodo Dragon

Here be creatures
    ten feet long
Here be beasts
    immense and strong
Here be huge and
    brawny tails
Here be skin
    with brownish scales

Here be brutes
    who overpower
Here be monsters
    that devour
Here be jaws
    with lethal bites
Here be giant
    appetites

Here be kings
    from days of old
Here be tales
    the ancients told
Here be teeth
    of dinosaurs
Here be feet
    with razor claws

Here be foul
    and fetid breath
Here be eyes
    as cold as death
Here be legends
    newly born
Here be dragons...
    you've been warned!

Graham Denton

I'm a Giraffe

I'm a giraffe,
with my head in the sky —
watch me stretch my neck up high.

I'm a kangaroo,
with my legs so strong —
watch me as I bounce along.

I'm a chimpanzee,
with my hands down low —
swinging my arms wherever I go.

18

I'm a snake,
with my body on the ground —
watch me as I slither around.

I'm a rabbit,
with my ears that flop —
everybody knows how to bunny hop.

I'm a crocodile,
with my jaws open wide —
why don't you come and look inside?

Mike Jubb

Hungry Crocodile

Float, float, float, hidden by the boat,
Is the hungry crocodile,
Scales, scales, scales, from the nose to the tail
Of the hungry crocodile,
Stare, stare, stare, goes the scary glare
Of the hungry crocodile,
Smack, smack, smack, goes the crinkly back
Of the hungry crocodile.
Scratch, scratch, scratch, goes the long claw catch
Of the hungry crocodile.
Snap, snap, snap, goes the sharp tooth trap
Of the hungry crocodile
SNAP!

Actions for you and your friends:

Line 1:   Pretend to float, fingers "rippling" under your chins.
Line 3:   Point to your noses, then to your feet.
Line 5:   Stare with menace!
Line 7:   Wriggle your tails!
Line 9:   Pretend to scratch with curled fingers.
Line 11: Stretch out your arms, then bring your hands together on each "snap" like jaws!
Line 13: Make one last, almighty SNAP!

Coral Rumble

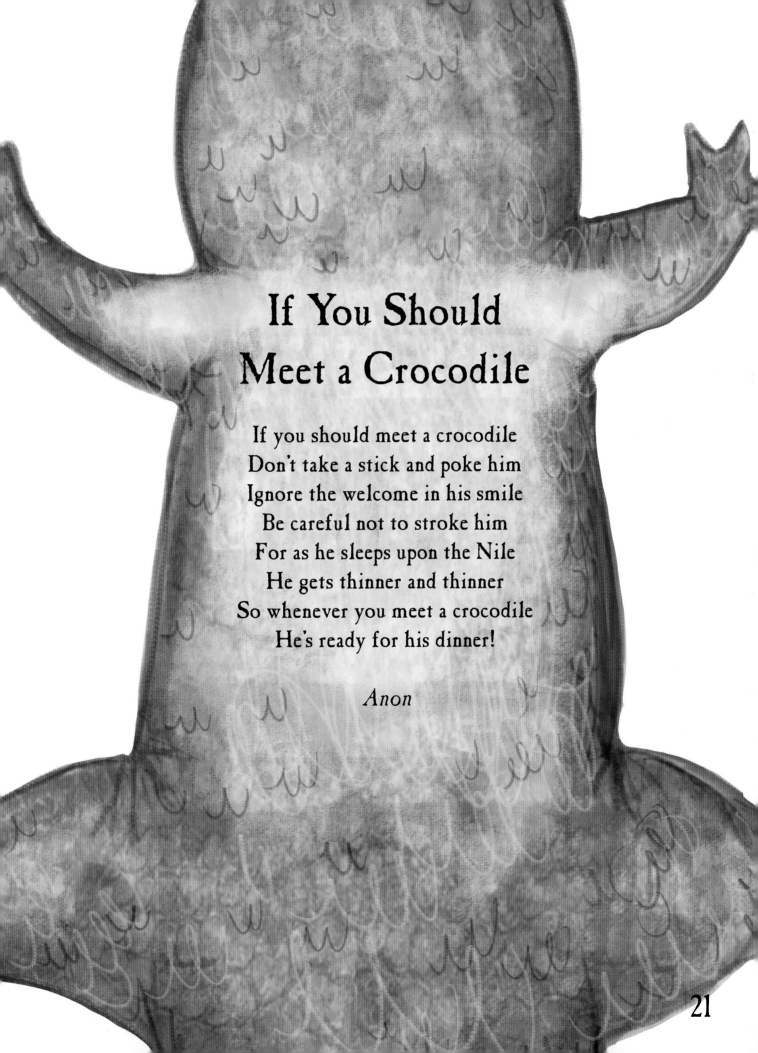

If You Should Meet a Crocodile

If you should meet a crocodile
Don't take a stick and poke him
Ignore the welcome in his smile
Be careful not to stroke him
For as he sleeps upon the Nile
He gets thinner and thinner
So whenever you meet a crocodile
He's ready for his dinner!

Anon

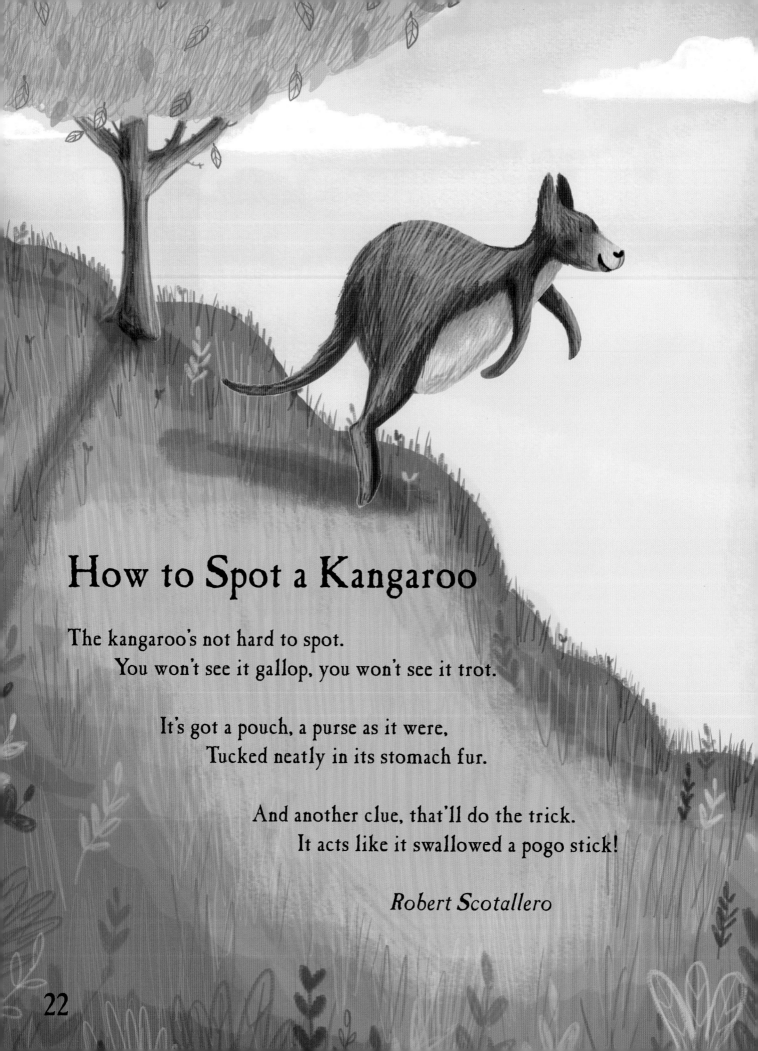

How to Spot a Kangaroo

The kangaroo's not hard to spot.
        You won't see it gallop, you won't see it trot.

    It's got a pouch, a purse as it were,
        Tucked neatly in its stomach fur.

        And another clue, that'll do the trick.
            It acts like it swallowed a pogo stick!

                                Robert Scotallero

22

Caterpillar

Brown and furry
    Caterpillar in a hurry,
Take your walk
    To the shady leaf, or stalk,
Or what not,
    Which may be the chosen spot.
No toad spy you,
    Hovering bird of prey pass by you;
Spin and die,
    To live again a butterfly.

Christina Rossetti

Swish Swash!

Up before the wallabies,
up before the gnus.
In and out and all about
through the caribous.

Polishing an elephant,
flossing a giraffe,
tick-a-ling hyenas
just to get a laugh.

Swishing and swashing,
underneath the minks.
Swishing and swashing,
"Morning, Mister Lynx."

Dabbing spot remover
on a leopard's tail,
vacuuming the feathers
of a nightingale.

Buffing up the pandas,
laundering the bats,
stop to pat a platypus,
scale the mountain cats.

Swishing and swashing,
under the impala.
Swishing and swashing,
"Pardon me, Koala."

Brush a little harder —
got to get it right —
can't have a crocodile
whose teeth aren't white.

Tidy up the antelope,
manicure the bear,
spring-clean the ceiling
of the old wolf's lair.

With a swish and a swash,
and a golly, golly gosh —
what a great day
for an animal wash!

Bill Condon

Tiger

A tiger is hiding there, under my bed,
with a black and gold body and huge stripy head;
and when it grows dark he gets bolder, it seems,
for he climbs on my quilt and slides into my dreams.

The tiger's decided he's coming downstairs,
but his sharp claws will scratch all the tables and chairs,
and he'll go in the kitchen and eat all the cakes —
that's after he's finished the chicken and steaks.

When he's eaten, the tiger goes running outdoors
and he rolls on the grass and he stretches his claws,
and his purr is as loud as an engine, his eyes
are brighter than stars in the blackest of skies.

I talk to the tiger each time he appears
and I stroke his great head and I fondle his ears;
and my tiger's as massive as massive can be.
So why is it nobody sees him but me?

Alison Chisholm

Animal Farewells

In a while, crocodile
See you later, small pond skater
Keep it real, you cool seal
Gotta go, my chum rhino
All my love, my sweet friend dove
Happy trails, little snails
Hey, hang loose, my darling goose
Well, see you then, you happy hen
Chin chin, penguin

My best wishes, friendly fishes
Goodbye for now, big brown cow
Love your pajamas, you funky llamas
Time to set sail, you graceful whale
See you soon, sweet racoon
Love and hugs, little slugs
See you there, my lovely bear
Love you lots, ocelots
Time for sleep, my little sheep

Kate Snow

29

Further information

Websites

For web resources related to the subject of this book, go to: **www.windmillbooks.com/weblinks** and select this book's title.

About the Poets:

James Carter is the liveliest children's poet and guitarist in town. He's traveled nearly everywhere from Loch Ness to Southern Spain with his guitar, Keith, to give performances and workshops in schools, libraries, and also festivals.

Alison Chisholm gets inspiration for her poems from her twin cats, Byron and Shelley. When she isn't writing poetry, she's usually to be found reading it or talking about it. Recently retired, she's still trying to decide what to do when she grows up, but as long as it includes poetry she'll be happy.

Bill Condon and his wife, the well known children's author, Dianne (Di) Bates, live on the south coast of New South Wales, Australia. They are both full-time writers. Bill's work includes novels, short stories, and collections of plays and poetry. He was the winner of the Prime Minister's Literary Award in 2010 for young adult fiction. His latest book, *The Simple Things*, was short-listed for Australia's Children's Book Council Awards in 2015.

Graham Denton is a writer and anthologist of poetry for children, whose poems feature in numerous publications both in the UK and other countries. As an anthologist, his compilations include *Orange Silver Sausage: A Collection of Poems Without Rhymes*, *My Cat is in Love with The Goldfish*, and *When Granny Won Olympic Gold*. Most recently, Graham celebrated the release of the first full collection of his own funny verses, *My Rhino Plays The Xylophone*. He has also twice been short-listed for the UK's CLPE Poetry Award.

Eric Finney wrote a number of books for children including *Billy and Me at the Church Hall Sale* and *Billy and Me and the Igloo*. His poems can be found in many anthologies. He was fond of walking and nearly always returned from his walks with ideas for poems. He lived in Ludlow, England.

Mike Jubb's poems are widely anthologized and he has a picture book, *Splosh*.

Brian Moses lives in Burwash, England, where the famous writer Rudyard Kipling once lived. He travels the country performing his poetry and percussion show in schools, libraries, and theaters. He has published more than 200 books including the series of picture books *Dinosaurs Have Feelings Too*. His favorite animal is his fox red labrador, Honey.

Christina Rossetti (1830-94) was an English poet who published a number of books and rhymes for young children including *Sing Song* and *Goblin Market,* a fairy tale in verse.

Coral Rumble has had three collections of children's poetry published, and is featured in numerous anthologies. She often writes for CBeebies TV and Radio. In 2014, Coral's first picture book, *The Adventures of the Owl and the Pussycat*, written in partnership with her illustrator daughter, was long-listed for Oscar's First Book Prize. Michael Rosen has said, "Rumble has a dash and delight about her work."

Robert Scotellaro's work has appeared in dozens of anthologies in the US and in England. He is the author of three books for children: *Snail Stampede and Other Poems*, *Dancing With Frankenstein and Other Limericks*, and *Daddy Fixed the Vacuum Cleaner*. He lives in San Francisco with his wife, Diana, and his writing companion, a real cool dog named Addie.

Joshua Seigal is a poet, performer, and educator who works with children of all ages and abilities. He has performed his poems at schools, libraries, and festivals around the country, as well as leading workshops designed to inspire confidence and creativity.

Kate Snow has been a newspaper journalist, a pop magazine writer, and a book editor among other things. She writes poems for children with brain tumors for The Brain Tumor Charity. She is mom to Luke and Lily and her favorite things are writing poems for children (obviously), shopping, portrait painting, licorice candies, shopping, dogs, and brass bands (she plays the euphonium).

Roger Stevens is a children's author and poet who visits schools, libraries, and festivals, performing and running workshops. He's written lots of poetry books and stories and runs the Poetry Zone, a website for children and teachers. He lives in France and England (although not at the same time) with his wife and a very, very, very shy dog called Jasper.

Marian Swinger was born in Lowestoft, England, but now lives by the Thames in England with her partner, son, dog, and chickens. For as long as she can remember, she has always loved to paint and draw and to write stories and poetry. She has been a professional photographer for most of her working life and has been writing poetry for children's anthologies for the past thirty years.

Index of first lines